New Albany - Floyd County Public Library
3 3110 00265 6492

VALENTINE FOXES

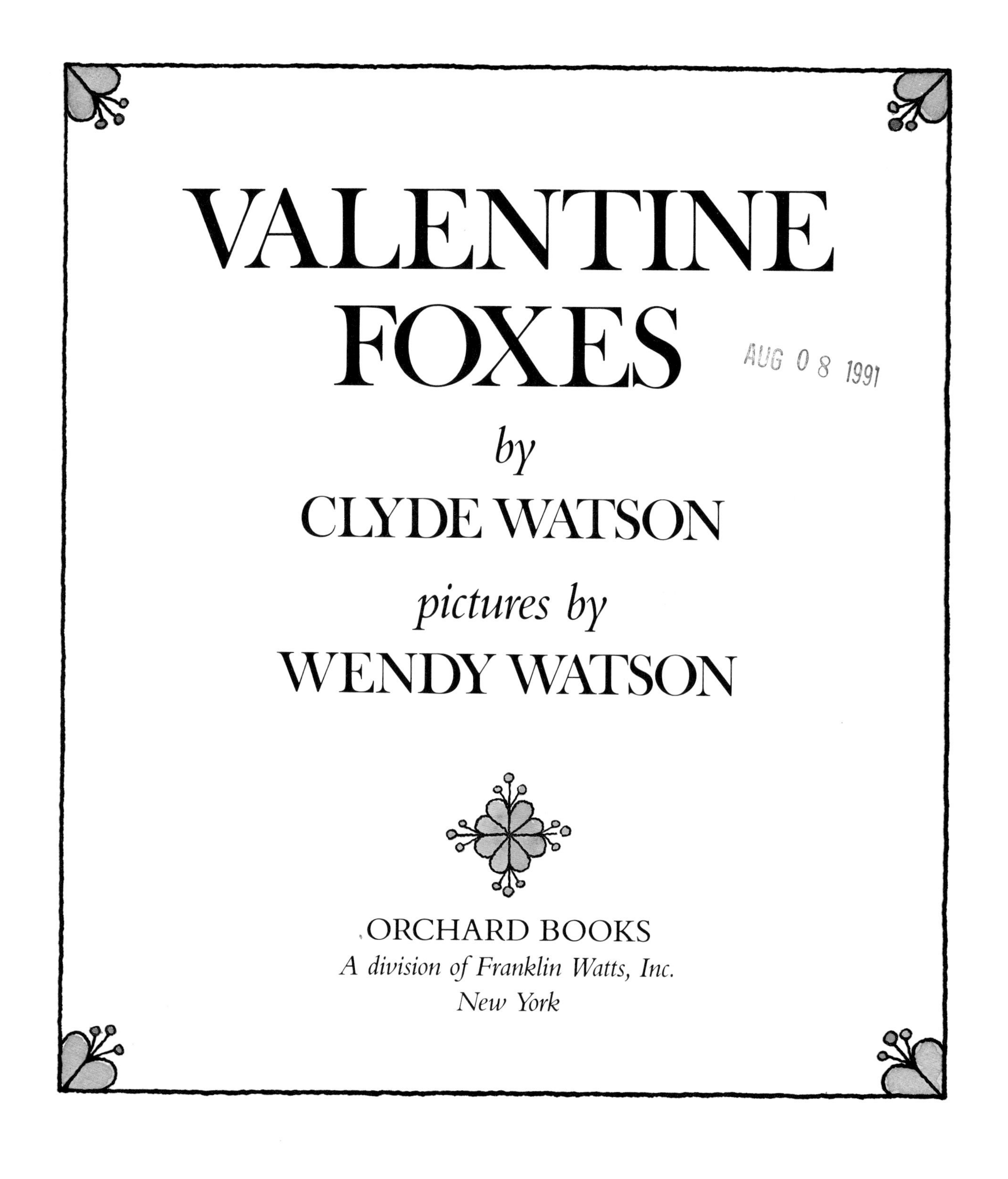

VALENTINE FOXES

by

CLYDE WATSON

pictures by

WENDY WATSON

ORCHARD BOOKS
A division of Franklin Watts, Inc.
New York

FOR DORA
WITH
LOVE
ELENA
EMILIO
MARIA

It was still quiet inside the Foxes' house, but the sun was already shining. Little Dilly woke up first—as usual—and she climbed up on Zandy, Pandy, and Poot, and woke *them* up, one by one—and then the four of them ran in and piled onto Mama and Papa Fox.

"Morning time!" they shouted.

"Happy Valentine's Day, little ones!" answered Mama Fox. She kissed them all and she kissed Papa Fox, who was still asleep.

"Oh Valentine!" she sang in his ear. "It's eight o'clock!"

"Whoops! Late again!" said Papa Fox, and he jumped out of bed.

"Happy Valentine's Day!" he said, and he kissed the little ones and he kissed Mama Fox. "Tonight I will come home early, but right now I'm late—so goodbye!"

And off he went, with his shirt on inside out.

"Valentine's Day?" said Zandy. "I know what *that* is!" And he whispered something to the others as they tumbled down to breakfast.

While the little foxes ate, they looked at each other and smiled about their secret. But Little Dilly was too little to understand, and she just sat on her banana and threw spoons, as usual.

Mama Fox whistled to herself as she cleared the table, and then she said, "I shall bake a wonderful cake today, and you can all make valentines, and when Papa comes home tonight, we'll surprise him!" So she got out her big blue bowl and put a cup of butter in it to soften.

Then she set the little foxes up at the table. She got out shiny red paper and lacy white doilies, glue and scissors and crayons. She showed them how to fold the paper to cut out hearts and other designs, and how to color doilies. But Little Dilly was very grumpy and fretful, so Mama Fox had to hold her and sing to her and bounce her and tickle her. But at least the butter was getting soft in the blue bowl.

Except that when Mama Fox went out to the kitchen to check it, Little Dilly leaned out of her arms and grabbed at the blue bowl, and down it fell to the floor and broke.

"Oh, my beautiful old bowl," sighed Mama Fox, picking up the pieces. "And the butter is ruined too. But never mind, I'll just run to the store for more."

So Mama Fox put on her coat and her hat, and went across the way to buy butter.

"Now," said Zandy, "let's work on *our* surprise. It will be for Mama and Papa—from all of us!"

So he cut out a very large paper heart, the largest one he could manage, and they all set to work. They colored some doilies and glued them all around the edge, and right in the middle, Zandy wrote "LOVE" with curlicues. They rummaged in Mama's work-basket and found ribbons and glitter and silver stars for decoration. The secret valentine was starting to look mighty fancy! Except that Little Dilly kept doing her own things, like pulling off stars and putting them on again in the wrong places.

"Never mind," said Zandy. "She's doing her best. We have to let her help too, because remember: It's from all of us!"

They finished their secret valentine just in time and hid it away, and when Mama Fox came in the door they were only doing usual sorts of things.

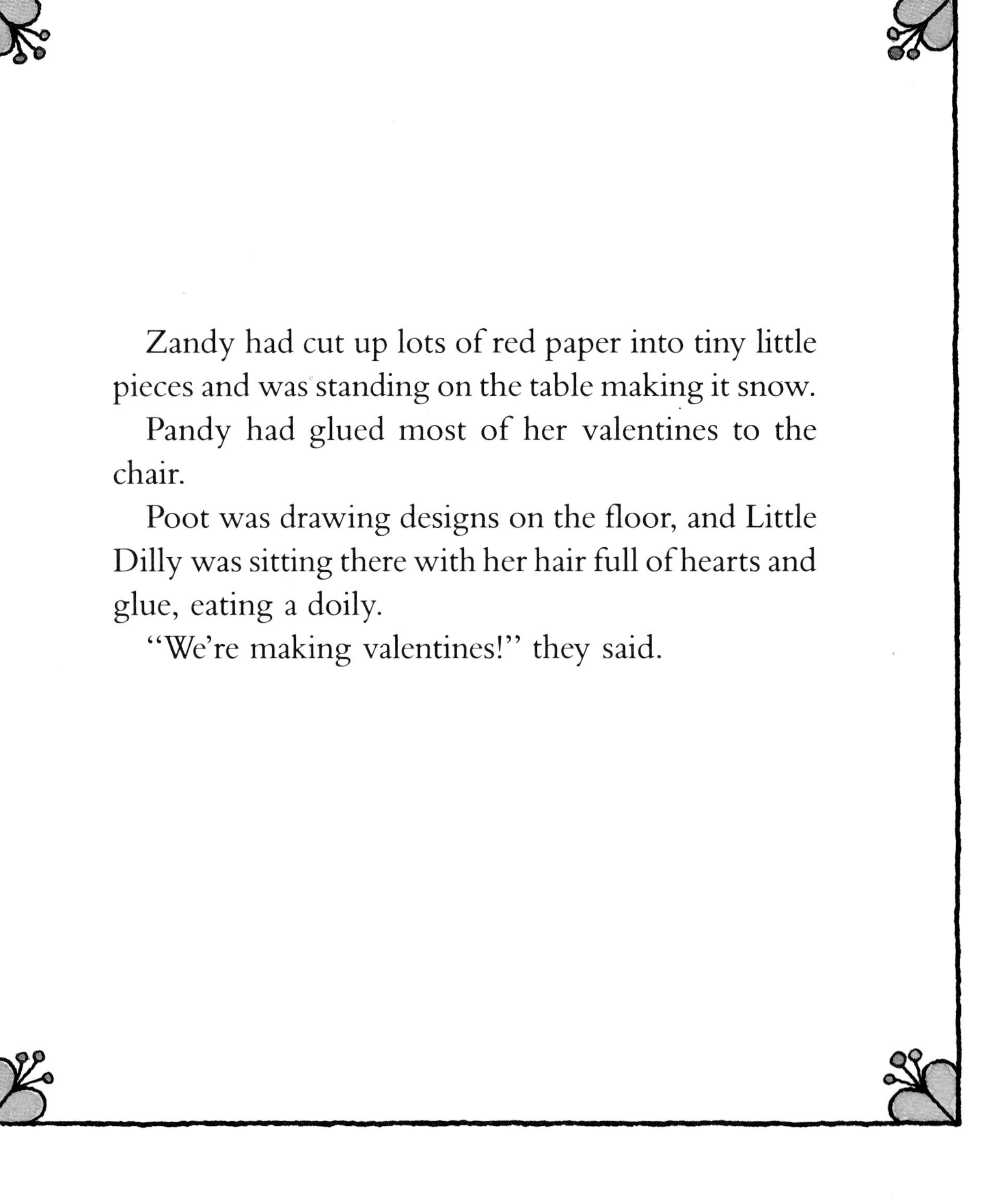

Zandy had cut up lots of red paper into tiny little pieces and was standing on the table making it snow.

Pandy had glued most of her valentines to the chair.

Poot was drawing designs on the floor, and Little Dilly was sitting there with her hair full of hearts and glue, eating a doily.

"We're making valentines!" they said.

"Oh, my little foxes," sighed Mama Fox. "The whole room looks like a valentine!"

And she went out to the kitchen to unpack her shopping bag.

"I'm hungry!" cried Zandy. "I want lunch!"

"Me too!" cried Pandy. "I want a cream cheese and honey sandwich!"

"I want mine right now!" said Poot.

And Little Dilly began to cry because she was hungry too.

So Mama Fox fixed cream cheese and honey sandwiches, and while the little foxes ate lunch (leaving their crusts) and spilled their milk and called for more, she got out another mixing bowl and put the new butter in it to get soft.

Then she opened up the cookbook and started to look at the recipe, but Little Dilly was all done in her highchair now and hollering to get out, so Mama Fox lifted her out to get her ready for a nap. On the way through the dining room where the little foxes were still eating, Mama Fox said, "We will *have* to clean this mess up somehow before suppertime!"

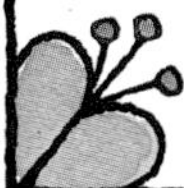
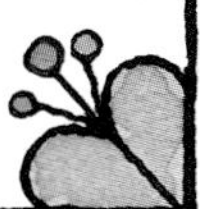

When she was gone, Zandy said, "Poor Mama—she *is* having a hard time getting that cake made. I say let's surprise her and do it while she's upstairs."

So *he* got up onto the stool to read the recipe, and the others climbed up onto the counter to reach things down and put them in.

"Sugar and eggs and a pinch of salt—that's what Mama puts in her cakes!" said Zandy. "And now: F for...flour, M for milk, and...this long word must be cinnamon!"

It was starting to taste like pretty fine cake batter! Except that one word in the recipe didn't make any sense.

"Let's see, V for...varnish? Or vitamins? Or... what *does* start with V that's nice in cakes?" asked Zandy.

"Vinegar!" said Poot.

"Whoever heard of vinegar in a cake?" said Pandy.

"Besides, there isn't any," said Zandy.

So they put in a few more spoonfuls of sugar instead.

When Mama Fox came downstairs Little Dilly was with her—"She would not go to sleep!" said Mama Fox.

She seemed quite surprised when she saw the kitchen.

"We made the cake, Mama!" said the little foxes.

"Goodness, little ones!" she answered. "You certainly did a lot in a short time. Papa is coming very soon—and won't he be surprised!"

Mama Fox looked at the bowl of batter, and she looked at the clock, and she looked at her little foxes all covered with flour.

"Did you measure?" she asked. "Did you follow the recipe?"

"Yes," answered Zandy, "kind of. Except for this one thing. We used extra sugar instead."

"Well," said Mama Fox, looking doubtfully at the bowl of batter again, "there isn't time to start all over. I guess we'll just have to hope for the best."

So she poured the batter into the cake pan and put the pan into the oven.

"Now," she said, "we *have* to clean up the dining room a little bit. Otherwise it won't look nice!"

While she put the soup on to heat up, the little foxes suddenly thought of something in the other room.

“Where is *our* secret?” whispered Zandy. They looked and looked all over the place, but it was nowhere to be seen.

“We have to find it before Papa gets here!” cried Pandy.

“Now we won’t have a valentine for Mama and Papa,” said Poot. “What shall we do?”

But just then Mama Fox came in.

"Quick!" she said. "I don't see anybody cleaning up! Papa will be home any minute!"

"But Mama," said Zandy, "we don't want to wake the baby up!"

For you see, Little Dilly had finally fallen asleep, right on the floor.

"Well then," said Mama Fox, "never mind picking up—just step around her and set the table, all right?"

So they did. They set the table with flowers and candles and place cards *and* a bowl of apples, and it was starting to look truly special. Except that the little foxes were really sad, because now they had nothing at all for Mama and Papa.

"Happy Valentine's Day, foxes!" called Papa's voice at the door. And in he came, with his arms full of mysterious little red and white packages tied up with gold string!

"What *sad* faces!" said Papa Fox, when he saw his children.

"Whatever is the matter, little ones?" asked Mama.

And Zandy, Pandy, and Poot began to cry.

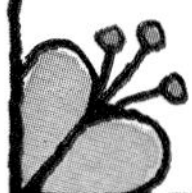

They made so much noise all crying at once that they woke up Little Dilly, and she began to cry too. It was starting to look like a not so happy Valentine's Day supper!

LOVE

Except that when Little Dilly crawled out from under the table, guess what: There was the secret valentine, stuck to her shirt! She had been sleeping on it the whole time!

"Happy Valentine's Day, Mama and Papa!" shouted all the little foxes, and they dried their tears.

Then Mama Fox lit the candles and brought in the

soup, and they all opened their presents. And when the cake finally came out of the oven, it tasted light and extra sweet and absolutely wonderful—even without the vinegar.

Valentine Pound Cake

preheat oven to 325°

Ingredients:

1 cup butter
2 cups granulated sugar
4 eggs
1 teaspoon vanilla (not vinegar!)
½ teaspoon salt
½ teaspoon baking soda
2¼ cups unsifted flour
½ cup milk
¼ cup applesauce
½ teaspoon cinnamon

Equipment:

1 large mixing bowl
1 small mixing bowl
measuring cup
measuring spoons
9-inch heart-shaped pan
or
6-cup loaf pan

Cream the butter and sugar until fluffy. Beat in the eggs one at a time. Combine the salt and baking soda with the flour. Stir half of it into the egg, sugar, and butter mixture, add the milk, and stir in the other half of the flour mixture. Finally, add the applesauce.

Butter a 9-inch heart-shaped pan (or a 6-cup loaf pan) and dust it with cinnamon. Fill it with batter and bake for 40 to 45 minutes until a toothpick inserted in the middle comes out clean. Cool the cake in the pans for 15 minutes, then turn it upside down on a cooling rack.

The foxes served their cake straight from the oven, just cooled. For a different taste, glaze while warm with the following glaze:

1¼ cup confectioner's sugar
¼ cup lemon juice
1 teaspoon vanilla

Combine these ingredients in a small bowl and spread the liquid immediately on the top of the warm (not hot) cake.

Clyde Watson lives in Hanover, New Hampshire, with her husband and two children. Her sister Wendy lives in nearby Topsham, Vermont, with her husband and two children. In addition to writing and illustrating, the two sisters play together in a string quartet that meets once a week.

ORCHARD BOOKS
387 Park Avenue South
New York, New York 10016

ORCHARD BOOKS CANADA
20 Torbay Road
Markham, Ontario 23P 1G6

Orchard Books is a division of Franklin Watts, Inc.

Manufactured in the United States of America

10 9 8 7 6 5 4 3 2 1

The text of this book is set in 14 pt. Bembo (slightly enlarged). The illustrations are watercolor and pen and ink

Library of Congress Cataloging-in-Publication Data

Watson, Clyde.
Valentine foxes / by Clyde Watson ; illustrated by Wendy Watson.
p. cm.
Summary: Four little foxes prepare a cake and a Valentine surprise for their parents.
ISBN 0-531-05800-X ISBN 0-531-08400-0 (lib. bdg.)
[1. Foxes—Fiction. 2. Valentine's Day—Fiction.] I. Watson, Wendy, ill. II. Title.
PZ7.W3263Val 1989
[E]—dc19

88-22392
CIP
AC